Hello reader,

My name is Olivia and I am 10 years old. Before we start the story I want to say thanks to my family. Without them none of this would have happened.

This is my very first book and I love writing stories at school. I am thrilled to have you read it!

I think every child loves a story and I hope to inspire others to write their own stories, no matter your age, you can follow your dreams.

From Olivia (the writer of this book)

FIRST EDITION

Monster Room

By O Smith

One day I was sitting in my bedroom, eating burgers, discarding the burger wrapper onto the floor with all the other rubbish, when mum came in.

"Tidy your room please Jack." Asked mum kindly.

"Why should I?" I sneered.

"Otherwise Monster Room may come." Replied Mum.

I thought for a moment, I was scared of monsters but I knew they weren't really real.

Mum kept begging me to tidy up my room but I kept refusing. No one makes me do something.

As night fell I heard a grumble, then a rumble, and then a monster seemed to spout from the floor, like it was coming out of my thick carpet and rubbish pile!

"W-W-who are you?" I stammered.

"I am Monster Room and I am here to make you tidy your room!" Announced Monster Room proudly.

"Noooooooooooooo!" I screamed. Perhaps monsters are real I thought starting to quickly tidy my room.

Every time I rolled my eyes or put something in the wrong place I got flicked in the ear by Monster Room, who looked like they were holding back a laugh, or wanted to flick my ear again!

Finally it was done and I flopped in to bed.

I watched Monster Room go out of my bedroom door. That's strange I thought, where is Monster Room going now.

Secretly I followed Monster Room down the stairs, who then took off their mask and revealed... MUM!

Printed in Great Britain
by Amazon